The Adventure Tree
Branch II
"The Royal Magic Show"

1

To order additional copies of this book, contact:
Xlibris
844-714-8691
www.Xlibris.com
Orders@Xlibris.com

ISBN: Softcover   978-1-4134-7448-0
         Hardcover   978-1-4134-7449-7

Library of Congress Control Number: 2004098316

Print information available on the last page

Rev. date: 08/31/2021

This book is for Scotti J.

Thank you for your love and encouragement
through a decade of "adventures" together.

To my young readers…

You'll never know where your special talents may take you,
if you don't share them with anyone.

Kelly

To my Readers:

Thank you for continuing the journey with Willow and Zak. I am so pleased to see them on another adventure.

My hope for all children who read "*The Adventure Tree*" books is that they will be encouraged and want to share their gifts and talents with others. I want children to plant seeds of kindness wherever their travels take them.

My promise to parents who purchase books in my series is that you will always feel good about having your children and loved ones read them. They will always be fun and exciting but above all continue to teach valuable lessons in life that will help them for years to come.

My dream for my books is not only to become a favorite of children, but also to become a classic to be enjoyed for generations.

Most sincerely,
Kelly

6

"Oh Willow, you do think our tree is still there don't you?" "Of course Zak, trees don't just disappear."

"But Willow, ours isn't just any tree, it's a magical tree." "What?" "There's no such thing as a magical tree. Let's just say that our tree is . . . hmm . . . special."

Zak looked up and smiled, "If you say so."

Willow looked right then left then right again, "It should be right around here somewhere. I'm sure of it."

"No Willow, I remember, it was further up."

Willow now turned to her little brother, and smiled while rubbing the top of his head. "If you say so."

After a few more feet of walking, they both stopped and gasped with air. The excitement of seeing their big, beautiful tree made their heart beat so fast.

"Look Zak, you were right. There it is!"

"Wow!" Zak squealed. "It looks even bigger than before, doesn't it?"

"You're right again."

A wide-eyed Zak asked, "Willow, what kind of tree do you think that is?"

Willow scratched her head. "Hmm, well . . . it's an adventure tree."

"Yeah." Zak giggled. "Should we climb it again?"

"Let's go!" they shouted together.

They laughed with delight the whole way up the big, strong trunk. There were many large, beautiful branches and it felt as if the tree was happy to have the children back.

"Look at this branch!" Willow pointed to a particularly large one over to the right. "Let's walk on it. It's covered by clouds so who knows where it will lead."

Willow began to run and Zak followed closely. They ran and ran until Willow got ahead of Zak until he could no longer see her.

"Willow, where are you?" Zak ran faster and the clouds made it difficult to see anything. "Willow! I can't see you."

Willow stopped and realized that Zak wasn't behind her. As she turned to look for him, he crashed right into her, knocking them off the branch.

"Oh no!"

12

The clouds were so thick they couldn't see where they were falling. As the children waved their arms and yelled for help, they stopped as they realized they were now flying upward. They held on tight to each other and as the clouds slowly moved away, they realized they were floating.

Zak screamed. "Wow!" "We're in a hot air balloon!"

Willow opened her eyes. "Oh my goodness, we are!"

"Woo Hoo, look at us Willow!"

They could hardly believe that they were indeed floating in a big, beautiful balloon.

As they jumped for joy, two birds flew by and chirped happily, "Hello children."

The kids sang right back, "Hello birdies, goodbye birdies."

They began to float down towards a beautiful village with cobblestone streets filled with shopkeepers sweeping the fronts of their stores and a group of jugglers next to a glistening fountain in the middle of town. A little further away, they spotted a magician entertaining a group of townspeople.

"Look Willow, a magician."

Willow looked with wide, excited eyes at the magician who was taking a bow. The townspeople were clapping, smiling and shaking their heads in amazement at the talented man. The children drifted a little further where they spotted an enormous, white castle.

All of a sudden they felt a sharp movement of the balloon.

Willow quickly grabbed Zak's hand, "Hold on tight, we're going to land. Don't let go."

As if the balloon sensed their anxiety, it gently landed on a patch of soft, overgrown grass.

Zak opened one eye, "Are we okay?"

They both glanced around and at the same time asked, "Where are we?"

They carefully stepped out of the big, gentle balloon and looked around.

"It's so pretty here." Willow whispered. "Let's take a walk."

They walked a short while when they noticed a man gathering sticks and flowers. As they got closer, they could hear him talking and it sounded as if he were telling a story.

"Excuse me, sir." Willow said very politely.

The man turned and appeared surprised to see Willow and Zak standing there. "Well. Hello there, were you speaking to me?"

"Yes, sir, I was speaking to you. My name is Willow and this little guy is my brother Zak. We just floated in on that balloon over there." She pointed to the soft ground where the balloon rested. "We're not quite sure where we are."

The man looked a little puzzled as he spoke. "Well Ms. Willow and Mr. Zak, you're in the small but glorious Kingdom of Avion. My name is Finneus and I'm the younger brother and chief assistant of the great magician Ezra. I'm gathering some props for some of his tricks."

"Oh, Finneus, Willow pointed out, " I think we spotted your brother Ezra entertaining a group of people just a short while ago. Do you also perform magic?"

"Who me? Oh goodness no, my brother is the real talent in our family. I could never be as good as him. I take care of his props and help him behind the scenes so his shows run smoothly."

Willow and Zak smiled at their new friend then Zak spoke, "My mother says we all have something wonderful to share with other people Finneus."

Finneus patted Zak on the head. "Thank you, but Ezra is the one who keeps our kingdom in amazement. I'm happy in the background."

Willow jumped in, "Hey, who were you talking to before? Was there someone else here?"

Finneus handed the children a group of bundled sticks. "No. There was no one else here but I like to tell stories to pass the time while I gather props. Sometimes, the animals nearby listen and I pretend they can't wait to find out what will happen next." He now passed some fresh flowers to them. "Do you think I'm silly?"

With props in hand, they giggled. "Of course not!"

"Thank you, I'm just about finished here. Would you care to walk with me into town? My brother will be performing a show shortly for the King and Queen. Would you like to come along?"

With excitement in their voices, they answered. "Can we?"

"Sure, it'll be fun."

Willow and Zak helped gather up the last of the props to help carry back to town. As they approached the kingdom, they saw Finneus' brother coming toward them.

"Hi Finneus, you certainly found some interesting props. Who are your friends?"

"Hello Ezra, this is Willow and her brother Zak."

"Great timing kids", announced Ezra. "I'm getting ready to go to the castle to perform a magic show for the Queen's birthday and I hope to give my best show ever!"

When they reached the beautiful castle, they found it was filled with people.

"Wow, the King and Queen really have a big family," said a surprised Willow.

Ezra agreed. "Yes, the Royal family is quite large."

Finneus started to set up the props in the Great Gathering Hall while the Royal children and guests began to take their seats. Anyone could see they anxiously awaited the magical journey Ezra would soon take them on.

Ezra spoke in a loud voice. "Greetings Royal Family, and a very happy birthday to you, your Royal Highness."

As Ezra began his show, the noise from the smaller children grew very loud, making it more and more difficult for Ezra to perform. He grew upset and frustrated as he saw the disappointed look on the faces of the King and Queen.

"Oh dear," sighed Willow. "This is terrible. There is so much noise, you can't hear Ezra."

Zak and Finneus shook their heads. "What shall we do?"

"I know!" yelled Willow. "Let's gather all of the children here in the next room and you, Finneus, can tell them stories while Ezra finishes his show."

"Oh no way!" Finneus said with a very frightened look on his face. "I'm way too shy, plus, I don't have any talent. My brother entertains people, not me."

Zak reached for Finneus' hand. "Finneus, we all have something special to share with others. You must find the courage to help or your brother's show and the Queen's birthday will be ruined."

Willow joined in. "Look! Children are running around and the props are getting knocked over."

Just then the magician's table fell over and crashed to the floor. The Queen stood up and looked very unhappy.

Finneus took a deep breath and whispered to himself, "I can do this." He cleared his throat and spoke up. "Your Majesty, may I request the pleasure of entertaining the children with exciting stories while you and Her Royal Highness enjoy my brother's magic show?"

The King paused for a moment, looked around at the crowd, and then nodded in approval. With a sigh of relief, Willow, Zak and Finneus gathered the children into the adjoining room where Finneus began to tell his fantastic stories.

The children sat in quiet delight and enjoyed every moment. Willow and Zak could hear the Royal family clapping and laughing in amazement at Ezra's tricks.

When the show was over, the King, Queen and Ezra walked into the adjoining room as Finneus was ending his story. The children roared with laughter and happiness.

The Queen approached the storyteller. "Finneus, the King and I are grateful to you for sharing your gift and entertaining the children while we enjoyed Ezra's magic show. Would you consider returning next week for perhaps another story hour?"

Finneus blushed as he addressed the Queen. "Yes, Your Royal Highness. I would be honored to return next week. I thank you for the invitation."

28

The Great Ezra put his arm around his brother. "Thanks Finneus, you saved my show and finally shared your stories with others. I've always told you that you're the best storyteller in the kingdom, but you didn't believe me."

Finneus looked happily at Zak and Willow. "I guess you're right. We all do have something special to share with others."

The King asked Willow, Zak, Finneus and Ezra to stay and join them for cake and ice cream. When they were finished, Willow and Zak went for a walk on the Royal grounds.

Zak hugged Willow. "What an exciting day! Let's sit here and rest a minute."

When they woke up they found themselves at the base of the tree and looked at each other with amazement.

"Oh Willow, I just had the best dream ever."

"Me too Zak."

As they began to share their dreams with each other, they looked down to find a sparkling magic wand on the ground between them. They smiled as they picked it up.

Holding the wand in their hands, they looked at each other and asked the question they may never really know the answer to. "Or was it a dream."

Printed in the United States
by Baker & Taylor Publisher Services